A passion for story time.

CW00420063

Andy Smart
2012

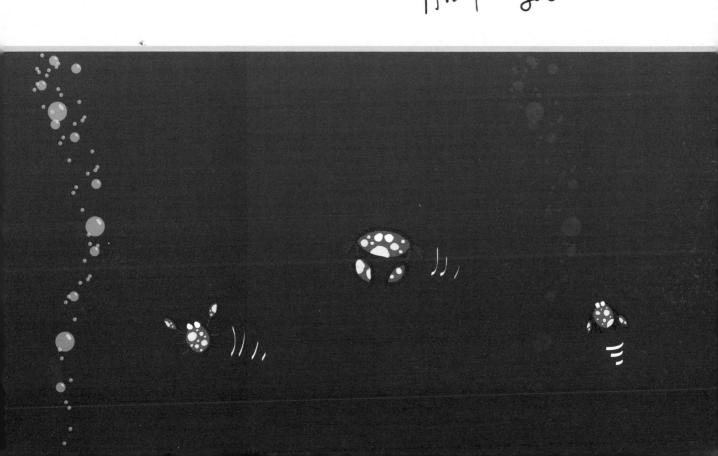

This book was given to:

_____

With Love, from:

_____

On this Date:

_____

If you'd like, would you say,
"Hi" to Joe, this beautiful day?
The sun is shining. The sky is blue.
I know that Joe would like to meet you

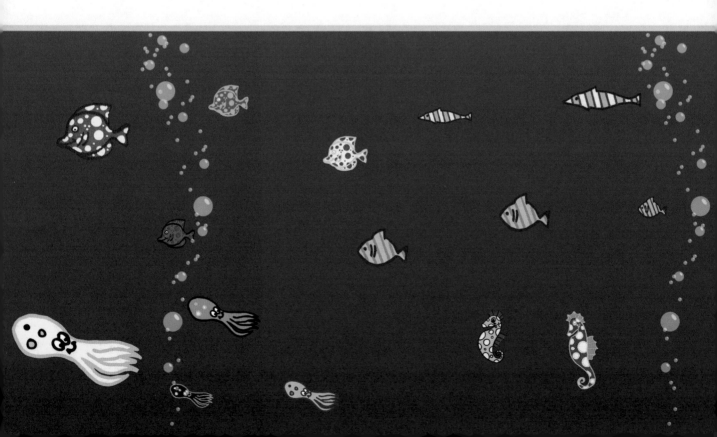

Joe is a kind and quiet man.
He lives in a boat with one plan.
To fish all day and fish all night.
It's one of his loves and he holds it tight.

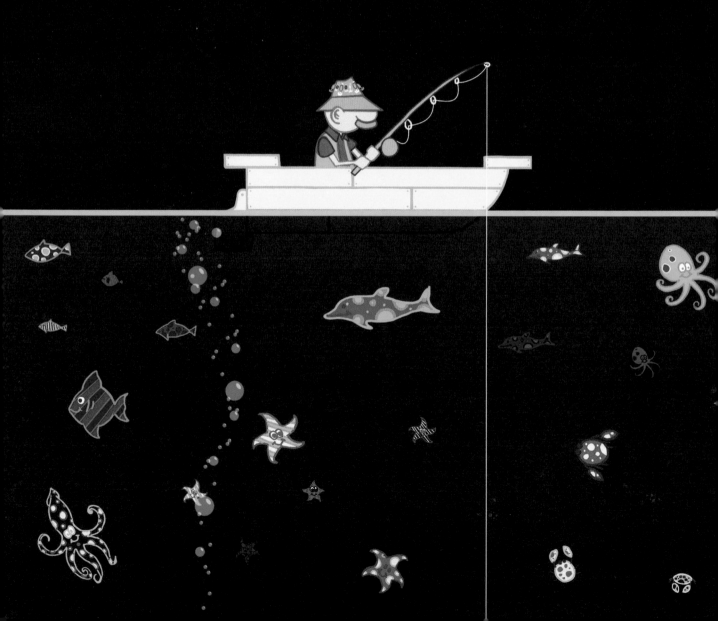

The second love that Joe knows best.
Is a sandwich he makes more often then the rest.
Bananas, honey and bread it takes,
to top with an olive, this sandwich he makes.

One beautiful day as his boat headed west.
Joe took out the sandwich he likes best.
It was sealed in a bag, safe and sound.
Keeping it fresh till lunch time came around.

At that moment along rolled a wave
And Joe's poor sandwich he could not save.
For up he was lifted and down he was dropped,
And out from his hands his sandwich popped.

As joe watched his sandwich in utter despair,
Along came a fish, who had jumped through the air.
With mouth opened wide the fish did eat,
Joe's lunchtime sandwich; A very tasty treat.

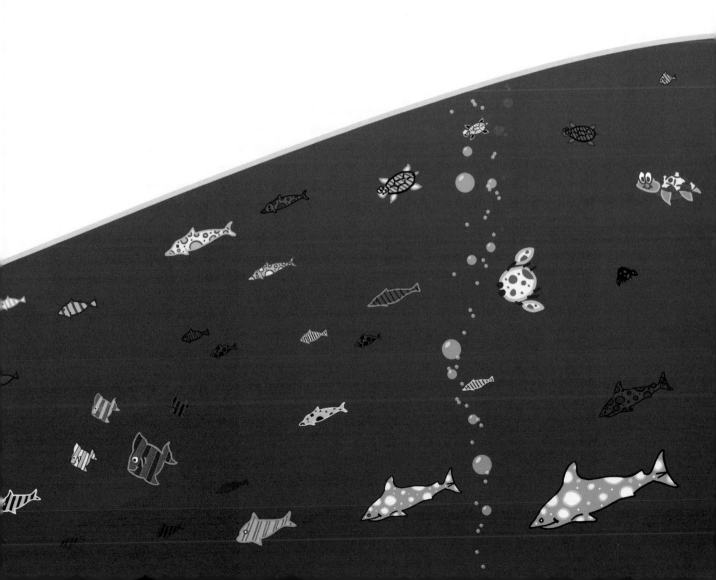

With a gulp and a splash gone was Joe's lunch.
What would Joe eat? What would he munch?
All that were around and close enough to see.
Had watched what had happened and didn't agree.

Now every fish and creature below,
Knew that Big Red had better run from fisherman Joe.
They were eager to watch as they knew what was next.
A game of cat and mouse that would be very complex.

Joe would not give up his sandwich, they knew.
Once he was ready his sandwich he'd pursue.
He opened his tackle box which rang a small bell,
Went straight for the shelf he knew very well.

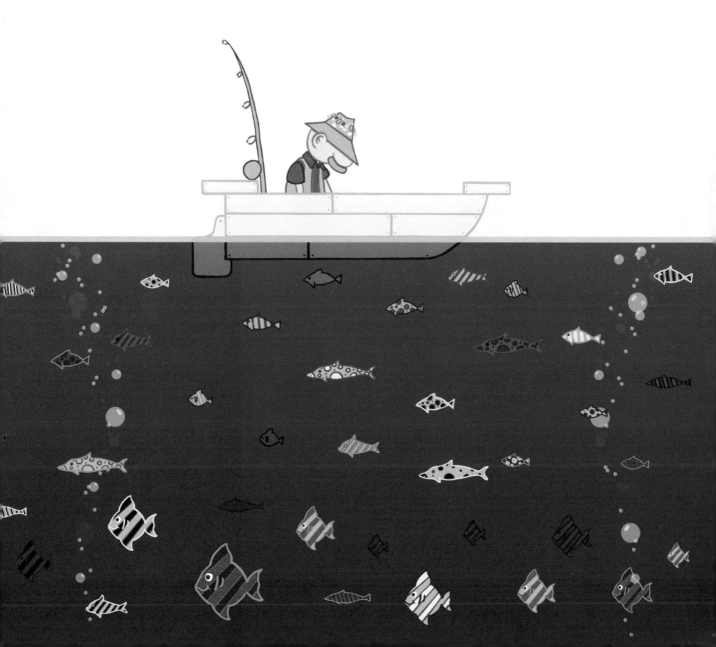

On this red shelf, special and clean,
You will find his BEST lures no one has ever seen.
Handmade with pride by Joe at night,
They are sure to catch Big Red, who was now out of sight.

Big Red didn't know this Joe very well,
Or he wouldn't have eaten that sandwich as he fell.
For as we all know and can speak very clear,
There are only two things that Joe loves out here.

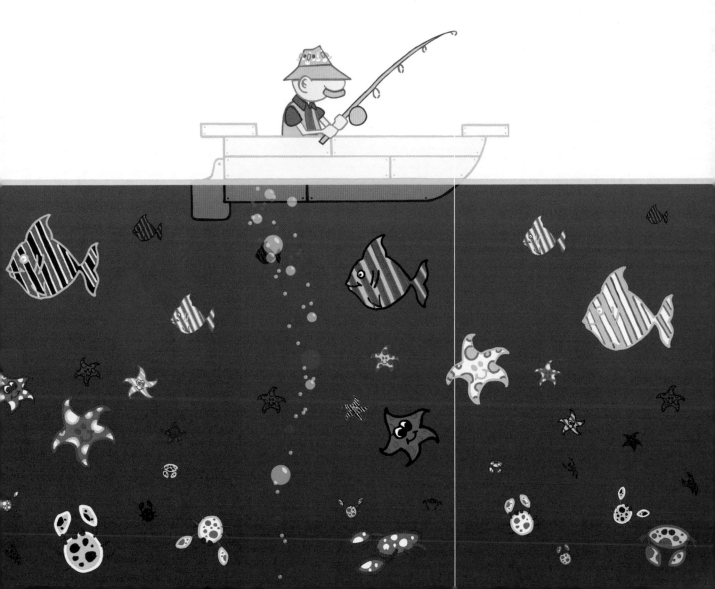

One is that sandwich in a tummy below,
The other is fishing; something Big Red will soon know.
For through good weather, rain and strong wind,
Joe never gave up, he just sat there and grinned.

For Joe knew at some point Big Red would not resist,
his best hand made lures, such a fish did not exist.
So confident and sure Joe continued his fight.
To retrieve his lost sandwich, Which was still out of sight.

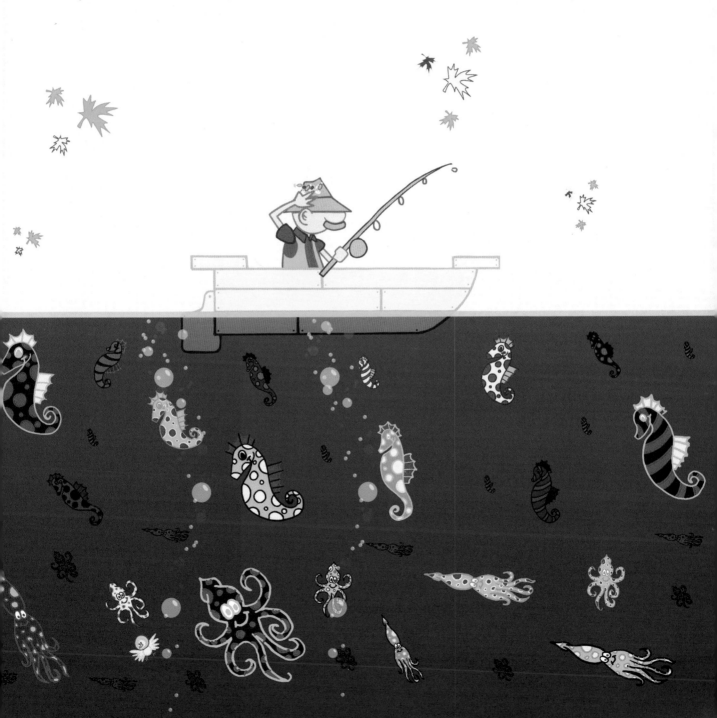

As surely as the sun rises each morn,
A fish of such strong will has never been born.
Soon tugs were felt on Joes fishing line.
He thought to himself "That sandwich will soon be mine."

Joe laughed at how easy this catch was to be.
He loved his good life out here on the sea.
So he prepared for his lunch. He would soon be eating.
He put on some coffee and started it heating.

One thing, very important, that Joe didn't know.
Was that Big Red was strong and he wanted to go.
So without warning or time to prepare,
Extremely fast was Joe pulled across the water up there.

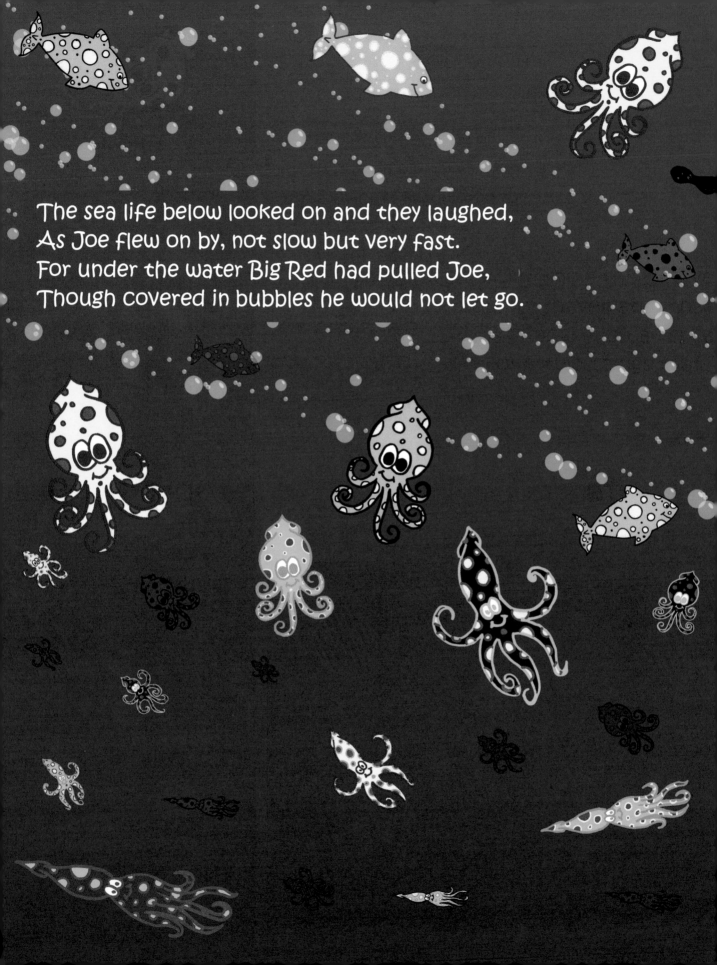

The sea life below looked on and they laughed,
As Joe flew on by, not slow but very fast.
For under the water Big Red had pulled Joe,
Though covered in bubbles he would not let go.

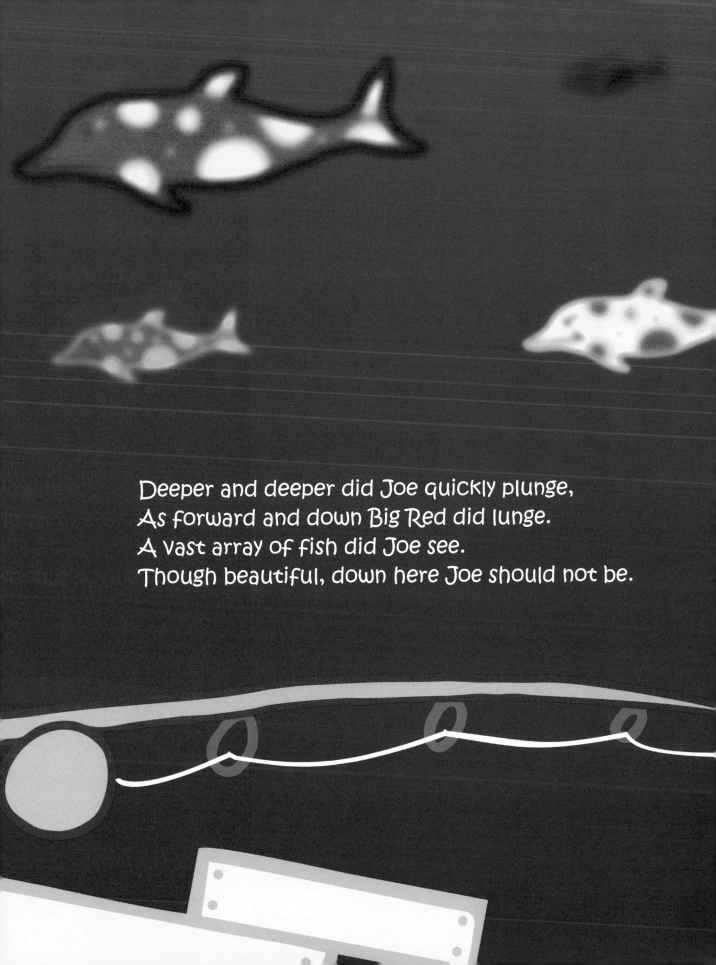

Deeper and deeper did Joe quickly plunge,
As forward and down Big Red did lunge.
A vast array of fish did Joe see.
Though beautiful, down here Joe should not be.

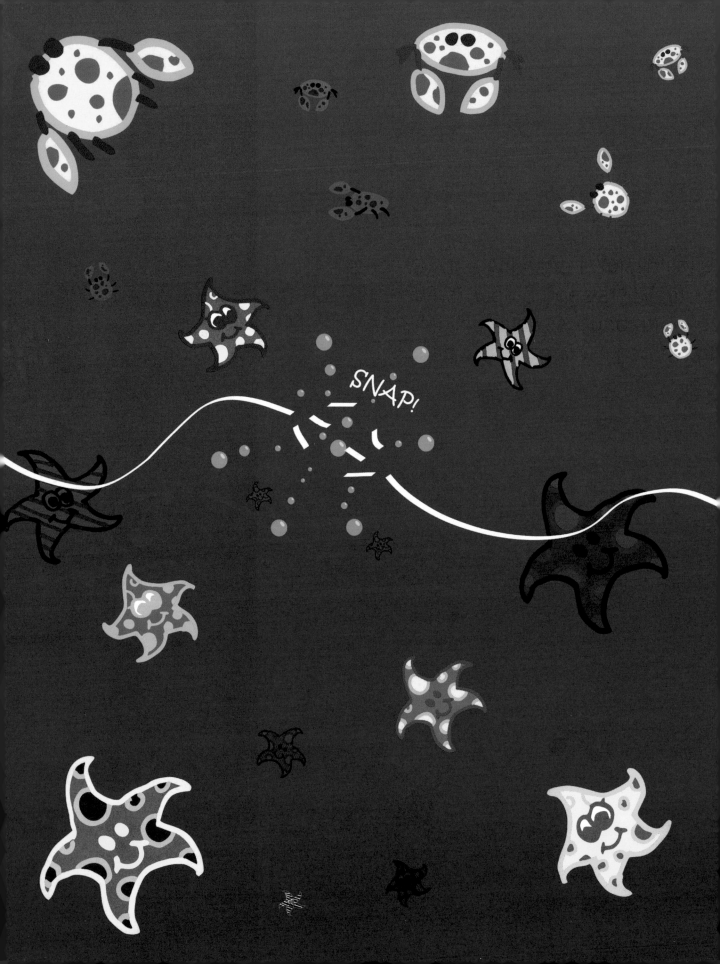

Suddenly and unexpected Joe's line did snap.
Under such strain, being dragged all over the map.
So up to the surface our friend Joe bobbed,
Feeling wet and somewhat royally robbed.

Did Joe give up his fight that day,
To retrieve his sandwich, as some might say?
We all know the answer and will cheer Joe on.
For Joe is our friend and his sandwich is gone.

Now as the end of this story draws near.
We say "Good night." to Joe, who's fishing out here.
We will see him again and join in his fun
but for now this story is done.

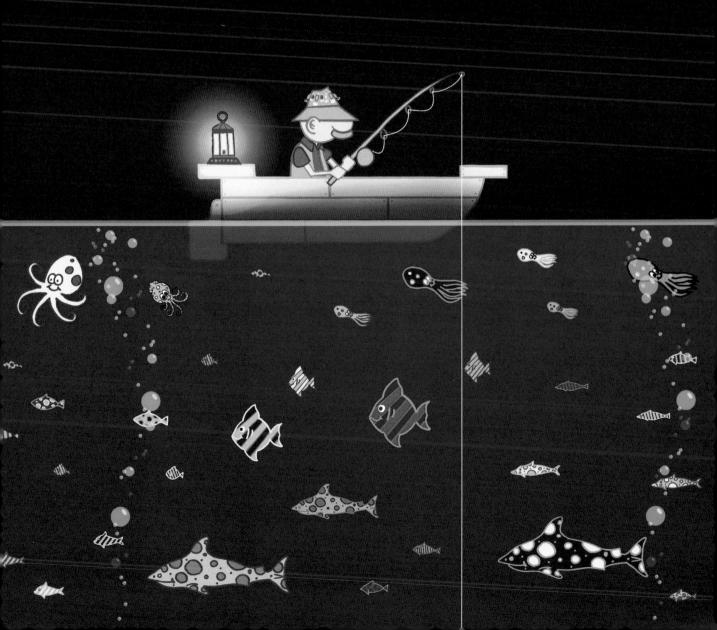

Have fun!

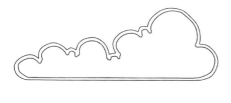
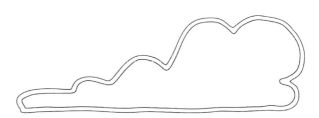

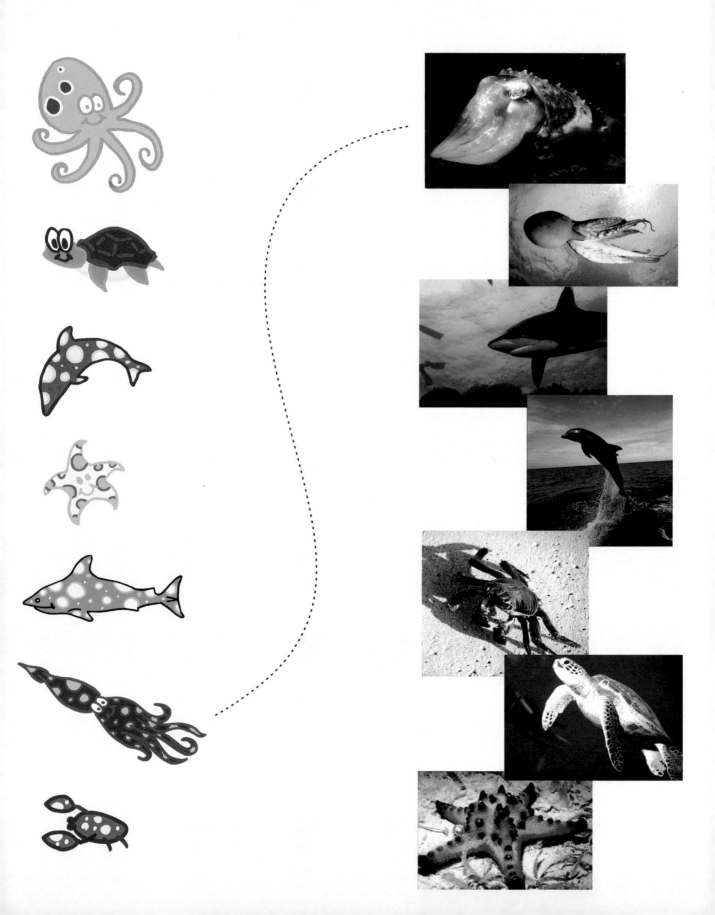

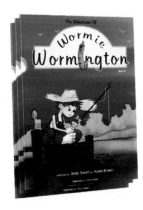  

To find more titles from Beckon Creative please visit
www.beckoncreative.com

Andy Smart has had a life-long love of great stories and artistic expression. This love guided him to study animation at Sheridan Collage in Ontario and Capilano University in British Columbia. In his heart, Andy has always been a classical artist. He loves to draw, paint, sculpt - any creative outlet he can get his hands dirty with. The computer has become another tool to create his vibrant artwork. Now it's his passion to craft stories that parents can trust and truly enjoy reading with their children.

Made in the USA
Charleston, SC
28 October 2012